# O Come, Emmanuel

# By Angie Lofthouse

O Come, Emmanuel
Copyright 2017

This is a work of fiction. The characters, names, incidents, and dialog are a product of the author's imagination and are not to be construed as real. Any resemblance to real people and events is not intended.

ISBN-13 978-0-9982792-3-7

Merry Christmas

From my heart to yours.

# O Come, Emmanuel

## I.

Morning came gray and damp, heavy with the scent of rain, mud, earthworms, and manure. Joseph Warren came out into the predawn to start his chores, but he let Peggy sleep. She seemed to need a lot of it with the baby coming.

The air outside the little farmhouse was still—too still—like all the sounds of life had washed away in the rain. The dripping of water off the rain gutters and the soft squelch of his boots in the mud were all Joseph could hear. His stomach turned fluttery. Nothing looked out of place, though. After a minute, he swallowed his unease and went down to the little pond to check on the ducklings. They might have hatched by now. That would surely calm his nerves.

The mother duck paced in front of the nest, quacking anxiously into the brooding stillness. "What is it, little mama?" Joseph murmured. He crouched to look into the nest.

The four ducklings were dead, their tiny, fuzzy bodies crushed, the nest obliterated. "Oh no." Joseph dropped to his knees, shivering. What could have happened to them? A predator would not have left the bodies here. They might have been smashed with a stone or stomped on hard, but that would mean someone…

No. No one had come to their hidden mountain homestead since Peggy's family all those years ago, and now it was just the two of them.

He scooped up the dead babies in his trembling hands. Blood pooled in his palm beneath their broken bodies. His stomach rebelled. "Yea, though I walk through the valley of the shadow of death," he whispered, trying not to puke, "I will fear no evil: for though art with me."

His racing heartbeat slowed a little. He searched the ground around the ruined nest for any clue as to what had happened, but found nothing. The rainfall would have washed away any tracks. It must have been an animal. A large one. Maybe an elk or a moose. That had to be it.

They were safe here. That's why his parents had come so long ago. So he'd be safe. Same as Peggy's parents. It was a safe place. It always had been.

He buried the little ducks in the soft ground at the top of a hill, near where his and Peggy's parents were buried, and set a smooth, gray rock—just a pebble, really—to mark the spot. "To everything there is a season, and a time to every purpose under heaven." Those were the same words he'd spoken at his father's grave. The same his father had spoken for all the others. Maybe it was a bit much for four tiny ducklings, but Joseph didn't care. It pinched his chest to think of them gone without ever getting a chance to live.

Finished, he stood and faced the other four graves. His parents and Peggy's had made their children safe, but they couldn't run from the disease that lived inside them. It didn't live inside Joseph, though, nor in Peggy. It wouldn't live in their children. At least, that's what Joseph's father had said before he died. Right before his final act on earth—joining Joseph and Peggy as husband and wife in the sight of God.

"Take good care of her, son," his father had said. "Don't ever leave this place. The Lord will provide whatever you need."

He'd been right too. Joseph and Peggy had everything they needed. But at times like this, when something awful happened, and his heart seemed to grow so large it filled his throat, he wished his father and mother were still here to reassure him that everything would be okay. He glanced down the hill to the farmhouse. What if something like this happened to Peggy or the baby? He turned cold at the thought. What if he couldn't take care of them?

But then the sun peeked through the clouds, the morning driving away the night's rain. Life returned to the little farm with the chattering of birds and a rooster crowing. Brown, the old dog, barked, and the sound of Peggy singing as she fed the chickens floated up the hill to where he stood, and chased away his melancholy.

"Joe!" Peggy called. "Where are you? The cow needs milking."

"I'm coming," he hollered down.

* * *

"That's so sad about the ducks," Peggy said, curling up against him in bed that night.

"Yes." Joseph sighed. He turned down the lamp, leaving them in darkness. The moon was hidden tonight. Joseph rested his hand on Peggy's belly. The baby squirmed inside her, and he smiled, but fear pinged against his heart. Thank heavens the darkness hid the look on his face from Pegs.

"Joe?" Peggy said in a whisper, "do you think we're the only people left?"

Maybe she'd noticed his fear after all. "I don't know." He kissed the back of her neck. "It's a big world. There are probably others."

"You think we'll ever meet anyone?"

Joseph couldn't tell if she was frightened or excited at the prospect. His stomach clenched a little at the thought. Then again—Peggy's family had once been strangers stumbling onto the farm. And look how well that had turned out. He snuggled tighter against her. "Maybe we will. If God brings them here."

Peggy was silent for long enough Joseph

4

thought she might have fallen asleep, but then she stirred. "I love you," she whispered.

He pressed his lips to her cheek, and felt the baby move again. "I love you too."

He closed his eyes, but long after Peggy really had fallen asleep, Joseph kept his ears pricked for the sound of footsteps outside the window.

* * *

Eventually, the silence lured him to sleep. It wasn't footsteps that woke him sometime near dawn. It was harsh pounding on the front door. Old Brown began to bark.

"What is that?" Peggy grabbed his arm.

"I don't know." Joseph's heart hammered as hard as the pounding on the door. He jumped up, fumbling in the dark for his pants. "Quick, Pegs. Hide. The root cellar."

"It's too dark," she protested. "I can't see anything."

"Just go. Hurry. You know the way." Joseph pushed her toward the window.

"Not without you." She clung to his arm.

The front door banged open and heavy footfalls shook the floors. Old Brown wasn't barking anymore. Why wasn't he barking? Flashes of bright light showed through the cracks around the bedroom door and outside the windows too. The farmhouse was small. The intruders would be in the bedroom any second.

"Peggy, go now." He watched the lights moving outside, praying it wasn't too late for her to get to the root cellar.

"Joe," she pleaded.

"I'll make them leave. It will be all right. I promise."

"No!" She tugged on his arm.

"Think of the baby," Joseph said. "Please go."

In the kitchen, crockery smashed against the floor. It sounded like they were overturning furniture in the front room and smashing the lamps. Who could they be? Robbers? Something worse?

Peggy clung to him for a brief, desperate moment. He kissed her fiercely and pushed her away. He pulled on his pants and grabbed the shotgun from the top shelf in their little closet. The bedroom door burst open with force enough to splinter wood, and the light blinded him when he whipped around with the gun raised.

"Drop it!" the voice was harsh and unnatural. Joseph couldn't see much around the light shining in his face—only dark shapes that held weapons of their own. He let the shotgun clatter to the floor.

"Put your hands where I can see them," the unnatural voice demanded.

Joseph thrust his hands out in front of him, barely able to breath.

"In the air!"

Joseph flinched, and raised his arms over his head.

"Down on your knees!"

He complied, his heart nearly exploding. His breath came out as hard as if he'd just run all the way from the creek at a dead sprint. Had Peggy gotten away? He didn't dare turn around to see. *Oh, please, Lord, let her get away.*

"Who are you?" He meant to sound brave, but it came out a shaky squeak. "What are you doing in my home?"

The men—soldiers?—robbers?—ignored his questions. One of them yanked Joseph's arms down painfully behind him and bound his wrists with something metal and cold, hard as a chain. The man wore a dark, hard covering over his body and a helmet that covered his face. Maybe that's why his voice sounded so strange.

"We have an illegal," the soldier said, though Joseph couldn't tell who he was talking to. "White male, approximately twenty years old. Blond hair, blue eyes. No visible defects."

That was him the man was talking about. What did he mean illegal?

"Bring him in," a new voice said plain as day from the man's helmet. "Continue to search the area. There may be more of them. Then collect and sanitize."

"Roger that."

Oh, the man—he did seem like a soldier—was talking through a radio. Joseph's father had talked to others on a radio when Joseph was a small child, but he'd stopped even before Peggy's family came.

*Peggy.* The soldier dragged Joseph to his feet and marched him out of the farmhouse. The other soldiers were taking food from the pantry and the ice box and loading into the back of a large truck. The cheese and bread, the fresh milk, and the eggs Peggy had collected yesterday morning. Plus the bottles of fruit and vegetables from their winter storage too.

"You can't have that," he protested. "Leave us alone."

He was rewarded with a slap from an armor covered hand to the side of his face. Sparkles of light swam in his vision and made his stomach sick, like the sight of the crushed duck's nest.

How could this be happening? He didn't see Peggy anywhere, thank the Lord.

The soldier marched Joseph up to the back of a second truck, where strong, ungentle hands lifted him onto the truck bed and shoved him onto a long wooden bench where more of the soldiers sat, their blank, helmeted faces turned toward him. The man next to Joseph pointed a rifle at him. "Don't make a move," he said in his radio-filtered voice.

Joseph stared back at his little farm being ransacked by the strangers. Maybe they were robbers after all. Robbers and warriors. The sun rose over the mountain peaks behind the house, painting the sky a soft pink. Where was Peggy? Was she safe? Would they find her? He wished he dared to make a run for it, but where would he go? He didn't want to lead these men to Peggy. Besides, he'd be shot before he even made it out of the truck. His arms hurt, stretched out behind his back. He squeezed his eyes shut, but when he opened them nothing had changed. This wasn't a nightmare, at least not one he could wake up from.

The truck rumbled into stinking life and pulled away. Away from the only home he'd known. Away from Peggy. Away from the baby he'd never get to see. Away from his parents and safety and the little paradise they had created for him. Despair lodged in his throat. The truck bounced on the little dirt path that led down the mountain, churning up mud and flinging rocks from under the tires. The bushes and wildflowers grown up around the edge of the path fell crushed and torn with the truck's passing.

The farmhouse disappeared rapidly as the truck descended the mountain, but just as the roof winked out of view, greedy flames rose to engulf it.

"No!" Joseph lunged forward. The man beside him yanked him back by the arm so hard he slipped, whacked his head on the edge of the bench and landed face down on the floor among the heavy boots and rifle stocks. Pain lanced through his head like a bolt of lightning. His vision dimmed.

He lay there on the floor and sobbed.

# II.

"Zeff! Zeff! Where are you?"

Zeff sat up, warm sand clinging to the back of his limbs. The murmur of the waves had lulled him to sleep, it seemed—a sleep full of dark and terrifying dreams. Monsters with hellish voices and no faces. Flames and panic. He touched the back of his head, almost expecting to find a knot there. A shudder rippled through his bones like the waves tugging at the sand.

"Zeff!" His little sister, Fern, came into view, waving her arms. "Come on. He's here."

Zeff jogged toward her. "Who's here?"

"The singer." Fern reached him and tugged on his arm. "Come on."

"Wait a minute." Zeff grabbed her arm to stop her rush. "Where's Plik?"

"Out hunting." She grinned. "He won't be back for days. He doesn't need to know the singer was here. And, anyway, Plik's not in charge of the village. Father is."

"Does Father know the singer has come back?" Zeff asked warily. The holy man's last visit had ended badly, with Plik shouting curses and warning the man not to return. Zeff had tried to stand up for the singer, but that had only made Plik angrier.

"Yes, he knows. He won't stop anyone from listening. Come on!" She tugged him forward. "You want to hear his songs, don't you?"

Yes. He certainly did. "Very well. Let's go."

"What were you doing clear out here anyway?" Fern asked

"Fishing," he answered guiltily. At least, he was supposed to be fishing, not napping in the sand. He couldn't say exactly why he'd ended up asleep. He'd gone down to the beach with every intention to fish, but instead…

Images from his strange dream flashed inside his head. Pain and darkness and fear, but more too. Strange looking trees and animals he had no names for. And the air had been cold there and dry. There? He shook his head. The whole thing was nothing but his own imagination, wasn't it? But he had seemed to be there.

He glanced back. His fishing nets and boat still waited on the shore. He'd have to come back for them later, and maybe do some actual fishing this time.

Zeff and Fern left the beach to hurry through the tall palm trees toward the village. Fan-like leaves of the deepest green left the forest floor in shadow. Monkeys chittered and hooted in the branches.

"See?" Fern pointed. A small group, smaller than the last time, had gathered around the central fire pit. The holy man sat on a stump at the head of the circle wearing a clean, white tunic and smiling at the people coming to sit around the fire and listen to his songs and stories. Zeff found Ivy, his betrothed, and sat on the ground beside her. Fern sat on Ivy's other side and took the hand of her sister-to-be.

When everyone was seated, the singer began as he always did, by singing the song of creation, accompanied by the beating of a small, skin drum. Zeff put his arm around Ivy, caught up in the spell of the man's words. He imagined the stars swirling into being along with the sun and the moon. If he closed his eyes, he could picture it. Endless pinpricks of light like precious gems scattered across a never-ending expanse.

Zeff joined his voice to the singing, along with Fern and a few others. He kept his eyes shut, letting the melody and rhythm spin pictures in his mind of the grandeur of God's creation. His heart rejoiced.

The song changed, as it always did. A hint of darkness and cold, evil slipping into the world, as unavoidable as the setting of the sun. That always made Zeff a little melancholy, but with the images of his dream still bumping around in his head, today it almost took his breath away.

Fern's voice faltered. Zeff opened his eyes and stopped singing as well. In a moment, all the gathered villagers had fallen silent. Zeff stood up, tense and ready to spring. His older brother, Plik, had come home after all.

## III.

Someone shoved Joseph out of the truck. He fell flat on his face without his arms to balance with. The back of his head still hurt where he'd hit it on the bench, and light sparkled at the edge of his vision. Thinking seemed too difficult. He wanted to close his eyes and return to the cool dark of the forest and smell the smoke from the fire and listen to the singing. But that wasn't real, was it? Had he dreamed it? He'd never seen such a place in his life. The clear, blue-green sea and white sand. The towering palm trees.

"Get up!" Someone kicked him in the ribs. Joseph groaned. He couldn't stand with his hands pinned behind him. He waited for another blow, but it didn't come. Instead, the metal bands fell away from his wrists, and someone helped him to his feet.

His benefactor was an older man, even older than Joseph's father had been. His hair was white as a puffy cloud and his face creased with wrinkles. He smiled warmly.

"I'm sorry for the unkindness you have suffered. Are you hurt?"

Joseph touched the tender spot on the back of his head. His thoughts came slow and sticky like honey, but not so sweet. "I don't—I don't know."

"Come with me," the kind man said. "We'll take care of you."

With his white hair and kind eyes, the man reminded Joseph of the holy man in the forest. He gave his head a little shake. No, that wasn't real.

The man took Joseph by the elbow and steered him toward a tall building of glass and steel. To either side, more buildings stood, more steel, and hard, black roads. Like the cities his mother had described with fear in her voice. He stopped. Maybe he ought to just run now. Try and get back home and find Peggy. Except they'd burned his home. Peggy was hidden. At least, he hoped she was hidden.

"Don't be afraid. My name is Morris. I'm a judge. That means I'm your friend."

A judge? Joseph nodded slowly. A friend. There were judges in the Bible, weren't there? What kind of judge was Morris? Could he get Joseph his home and his wife back so Joseph could take care of her and the baby?

There didn't seem to be any other choice but to go with him.

"What's your name, son?"

"It's Joseph." He winced at the pain talking caused his head.

"Don't worry, Joseph. I know you're hurt and probably frightened, but I promise it's going to be all right."

That's what Joseph had promised Peggy too,

and he had to keep that promise. He straightened his shoulders, trying to find his courage. It was going to be okay.

* * *

Joseph winced as the nurse sealed up the wound on his head with something cold and stinging. "You'll feel better in no time," he said cheerfully.

Joseph shivered and his stomach churned. He wanted his parents. He wanted Peggy. He wanted to go home. Weariness sat heavy on him.

Judge Morris stood on the other side of the room, leaning against a counter, waiting patiently for the nurse to finish. For Joseph, the man was a rock in the river, something solid to cling to in the turbulent confusion. The judge would take care of him. It would be all right.

"All done." The nurse patted Joseph's shoulder, and helped him down from the tall exam table.

"Feeling better?" Judge Morris asked.

Joseph nodded. The stinging had stopped and with it the pain. But it was still hard to think clearly. He still wanted to slip back onto the warm sands or curl up sobbing in Peggy's arms. He wanted Peggy back more than anything.

"Good. Let's go." The judge beckoned Joseph out of the room. He stayed behind the judge, keeping his eyes on the floor. Looking out into the bright sunshine made his head hurt again. The judge had his hands folded behind his back and walked in long, confident strides. He led them through thick sliding doors into a tiny, windowless room with no furnishings. Joseph hesitated.

"It's an elevator," Judge Morris explained. "To take us to the upper floors. Would you rather use the stairs? It's a long way up."

"Uh, no." Joseph stepped into the elevator, embarrassed by his lack of knowledge. He didn't want to look like some kind of coward. The elevator didn't make a sound carrying them upward. Joseph stuck his hands in his pockets. Judge Morris didn't speak. It wasn't long before the doors slid open to reveal a more fancy hallway than the glass and steel below.

Soft, cream-colored carpet lined the floor. Judge Morris opened a door of red-brown wood, and ushered Joseph into a large space with tall windows. A cozy arrangement of couches and easy chairs took up half the room. They all looked new and soft, not like the worn furniture in the farmhouse.

A desk of the same shiny wood as the front door dominated the rest of the room. Only a small brass lamp stood on top of it. Behind the desk was a bookshelf. Joseph's heart lifted a little. Maybe Judge Morris would let him read some of the books. He had so few at home.

*Home.* His heart dropped again. Home was

gone.

"Make yourself comfortable," the judge said. He sat on one of the easy chairs. Joseph chose a couch next to him. The cushions molded against his body, and he wished he could fall asleep. Sleep, and wake up in his own bed beside Peggy with this nightmare over. Tears crowded the corners of his eyes. He blinked them away.

Tell me about your farm," the judge said. If he noticed the tears, he didn't say anything.

"My...my farm?" Joseph swallowed the lump in his throat.

"How long have you lived there?"

"All my life," he muttered. "My father built it."

"I see." Judge Morris steepled his fingers and tapped them against his lips for a moment before he spoke again. "Did your father tell you why he built it?"

"Yes." Joseph took a deep breath to still the quaver in his voice. "He built it as a safe place for us. We...we wanted to be left alone." He stopped, pressing his lips together. Why couldn't they just leave him alone? He wanted to ask Judge Morris, but that might seem rude.

"A safe place. That's an admirable goal." Judge Morris stood up and walked over to his desk. Joseph watched over his shoulder. The judge opened a desk drawer and pulled out a familiar, well-worn, black leatherbound book. Joseph's Bible. Judge Morris brought it back over to the easy chair.

"My men found this in your house."

Joseph blinked. The cruel soldier's were the judge's men? But they burned his house—unless maybe that was an accident, or not what he thought he'd seen.

"Do you recognize it?" Judge Morris asked.

"Sure." Joseph reached for the scriptures, longing for their comforting, familiar feel in his hands.

Without handing them over, Judge Morris examined the name embossed in gold on the cover. "Michael Alan Warren," he read. "Is that your father?"

"Yes."

"And you've read this book?"

"Oh, yes. We read it every day." He held out his hand again. "May I…may I have it back?"

"I'm afraid not, Joseph." He set the Bible down on an end table. "This may be hard for you to hear, but you must trust me."

Joseph scrunched up his forehead, waiting. Judge Morris seemed less friendly suddenly, though he still wore a kindly expression.

"Reading books such as these is against the law," the judge said. He sounded like Joseph's father offering gentle reproof at Joseph's occasional rule-breaking. But reading the Bible? How could that be against the law?

"What do you mean—books like this?"

"Books of a religious nature. Books which claim divine origin."

"Why is that against the law?"

"Because these books and others like them have been used to justify the worst sorts of actions you can imagine. They encourage divisiveness and hatred, and they were outlawed long ago."

"I don't understand," Joseph whispered. He'd never felt any hate toward anyone from reading the scriptures—quite the opposite. His stomach hurt.

"I don't blame you, Joseph. I'm sure you only did what your parents taught you to do. Believed what they taught you to believe. Right?"

"Yes. I guess." It felt like a betrayal. His parents couldn't have been wrong, could they?

"Where are your parents now?" Judge Morris tilted his head to the side, genuine concern on his face.

"They…they…they died." Now he couldn't stop the tears from sliding down his cheeks. He wiped them away with his fist, ashamed.

"I'm so sorry. How did they die?" The judge still sounded kind, but his words jarred in Joseph's mind.

"They had a disease," he mumbled.

Judge Morris nodded. "McKutcheon's Disease."

Joseph swallowed. "They never told me the name. It lived...it lived inside them for a long time."

"Yes. McKutcheon's was quite devastating at first. Millions died. But you don't need to worry. We know how to cure it now, and we can vaccinate against it. It's a shame really."

"What is?" Joseph swiped at his eyes again.

"If your parents had not run away to this—safe place—they would not have died."

"Oh." Joseph's heart did an odd, painful little twist.

"Yes. You see, Joseph, your parents meant well, I'm sure, but they made a mistake. A horrible mistake." He picked the scriptures up from the end table, and set them on his lap with a sigh. "They made the mistake of believing in this." He patted the worn leather cover. "In believing there was a God."

"What are you saying?"

"There is no God, Joseph. That's just a myth. A foolish, childish wish."

Joseph spread his hands out flat against the couch cushions, trying to catch his breath. To think of something to say. The judge was wrong. He had to be. And yet—God had not prevented the soldiers from finding the farm, from burning it down. No. He couldn't accept it. His parents surely hadn't taught him lies. "You're...are you...You're antichrist."

21

Judge Morris chuckled. "Maybe so, but only because I want you to know the truth." He stood up, dropping the Bible back on the end table. "Let me show you something."

Joseph pushed himself up from the couch. Judge Morris led them over to the wide windows. "Look." The judge gestured to the scene outside. The window looked down on a tall cinder block wall with barbed wire twisted around the top. Beyond that, he could see buildings in ruin, burned and broken. Columns of smoke rose here and there. The entire scene was a blasted and gray wasteland. A few soldiers moved through the ruins.

"What happened to it?"

"War." The judge put his hand on Joseph's shoulder. "Did your parents ever mention the war?"

Joseph hesitated. His parents had often spoken of the danger of leaving the farm, of people who would try to hurt him. But they'd never called it a war. "No, they didn't." He looked out over the devastation feeling ill all over again.

"I'm sure they were trying to protect you, but there is a war—the whole world is at war. McKutcheon's Disease was just the first strike." He turned from the window and put his hands on Joseph's shoulders, looking him in the eyes. "People are suffering, dying every day. People are sick and hungry. Starving. Do you know who's going to take care of them? Who's going to put a stop to this terrible war?"

"No." Joseph balled his trembling hands.

"We are. You and I and every other person who remains in this country. Not some mythical god. We have only ourselves to rely on. No god has ever come down from the clouds to rescue us. We have to do that ourselves. Do you understand?"

Joseph stood silent, his mind reeling. That couldn't be true, could it? He shrugged, not trusting his voice.

"It's the truth." Judge Morris's voice was still mild, kind, but now it had a hard edge. He dropped his hands from Joseph's shoulder. "We all must take care of each other, you see. That's why what your parents did was so wrong. They refused to do their part. They hid instead of helping. They kept food for themselves instead of sharing it with the hungry. We cannot allow that to continue, you see. Not when we need every person to do their part. Not when we need food to feed everyone—not to be hoarded just for you."

Joseph hung his head, a sudden shame burning in his chest. "I didn't know."

"That's all right. It's not your fault. But now that you know better, you can do better. You can do your part to save all of us, can't you?"

Joseph nodded, but he couldn't look the judge

in the eye.

"I'm going to assign you a job where I need you most. I expect that you will do your best there, and that you will remember that together we can change all this, but only if we all do our part."

"Okay," he muttered.

"I want you to forget the lies and wrongful things your parents taught you." Judge Morris walked over to the end table and picked up Joseph's Bible—his father's Bible—and tossed it into a fireplace against the far wall. A fire flared into existence, the flames licking the leather cover of the book and greedily devouring the pages.

Joseph took an involuntary step toward it. Judge Morris put a restraining hand on his arm. "This is best, Joseph. For your own good and the good of everyone else."

Joseph watched the book burn. It was like losing all his best friends. Almost as painful as when his parents died. Almost as painful as not knowing where Peggy was.

"Joseph—" The judge's grip on his arm tightened. "This is important. Was there anyone else with you on your farm? Remember, we need everyone. Every single person."

His heart began to pound. "No. Just me." Maybe the judge was right, but Joseph didn't want Peggy exposed to this.

"You're wearing a ring." Judge Morris nodded at Joseph's left hand. "A wedding ring."

"My father's ring."

"Do you have a wife? Any children of your own? If you're trying to protect them, it won't do any good."

That must mean the soldiers hadn't found Pegs.

"No. I just—wanted to remember my father." He wasn't sure how he felt about Judge Morris or the things he'd said, but he knew for sure he didn't want Peggy's heart broken by the judge's words or the sight of the ruined city. *Heavenly Father, please protect Peggy and the baby.* He stopped. Was anyone even listening? He hated the doubt Judge Morris had put into him, but there it was.

Judge Morris stared at him, his expression stern. Joseph forced himself to meet the man's eyes. For Peggy's sake.

"You'll have to give the ring to me," the judge said. "Anything of value is to be used for the good of all." He held out his hand.

Joseph touched his father's ring, twisting it around his finger without pulling it off. Judge Morris kept his hand out, but didn't speak. Joseph's fingers trembled as he slipped off the ring and placed it in the judge's palm.

"Thank you." His fingers closed around the gold band. He moved over to his desk and touched

25

the surface. "Please send someone to escort the illegal to his new assignment."

"Yes, sir," a voice responded.

There was some kind of radio on the desk?

Judge Morris fixed Joseph in his gaze again. "Please understand, if you try to run away, to go back to the farm or anywhere else, you will be put to death."

Joseph swallowed. Put to death?

"I know it sounds harsh, but in our situation we cannot afford to make exceptions. Everyone must do their part."

Joseph looked down, wiping his palms on his pants. "I understand."

"The only reason I'm giving you this chance is because I know your rebellion wasn't your fault. You weren't taught the truth." Judge Morris sat down in the black chair behind the desk. "If there is anyone else who was on that farm with you, if you tell me now, I'll give them the same chance I'm giving you. But if we find someone there after another search, someone you didn't tell me about, I'll have to put them and you to death. There can be no exceptions."

Joseph's head went all light and fuzzy. Give up Peggy or risk her execution? But the baby—surely the judge wouldn't... The memory of crushed baby ducks floated in his head. Those were the judge's soldiers who did that. Who burned his farmhouse.

He balled his hands into fists. "I had…I did have a wife. But she died. She died having a baby." Up until today, that had been his greatest fear—that something would go wrong when the baby came.

Judge Morris folded his hands on top of his desk. "I'm sorry to hear that. It must have been difficult for you."

Joseph nodded mutely. Tears welled in his eyes again—shame over lying, fear that he would never see Peggy again, the painful realization that Judge Morris might be right about everything. Maybe there really was no God at all. If there was, it sure seemed like He had abandoned Joseph and Peggy.

"I want you to remember everything I've told you today," Judge Morris said. "You'll find your purpose here and you'll learn to be content with the part you must play in making the world a better place." His kind smile returned. "You've done the right thing today."

A knock at the door made Joseph jump. The door swung open and a woman in splotchy gray pajamas offered the judge a crisp salute. A uniform, Joseph realized. Not pajamas. She was a soldier too.

"This is Joseph Warren," Judge Morris told her. "I've sent you his assignment. Please get him registered and escort him there."

"Yes, sir." She saluted again. "Follow me, Mr. Warren."

Joseph looked once over his shoulder before he left the judge's office, and saw the fire turn the last bit of his Bible into ashes.

# IV.

"What's all this?" Plik demanded. His deep voice reverberated around the fire circle. "I thought I told you not to return, old man."

The singer stood, unruffled. "I was invited to sing when I passed through the village earlier."

"By who?" Plik stood nose to nose with the holy man, holding his bow in one hand. The rest of his hunting party stood arrayed behind him, all of them somber-faced and scowling.

Zeff stepped forward. "It doesn't matter who. You don't speak for the village."

Plik turned his attention to Zeff and his expression turned truly ugly. "Do you, little brother?"

Zeff threw back his shoulders. He wouldn't let Plik see the fear racing up his spine.

"Look at us," he told Plik. "Does it look like we don't want the singer here?"

"The singer." Plik scoffed. "Sitting around listening to foolish songs sung by a dreamer does not do this village any good."

"You don't have to listen," Zeff said. "You can go back to your hunting and leave us alone."

"Leave you alone?" Plik stepped toward him. The muscles in his shoulders bunched up like he was getting ready for a fight. Zeff flinched.

"You think our hunting is just some game? That we're not keeping this village alive?"

Zeff didn't answer. Plik was right about that.

"Peace." The singer stepped between them. "I would not bring discord to your village."

"Then leave," Plik said, still glaring at Zeff.

The singer dipped his head, and moved out of the circle, away into the forest without another word. Zeff's hands trembled with anger, but he didn't move. The other villagers stood also, quietly going back to their tasks. No one else seemed inclined to argue with Plik and the other hunters. Even Fern and Ivy got up and walked away together. Ivy looked at Zeff over her shoulder, her expression a mixture of embarrassment and disgust that hit Zeff like an arrow in the chest. Was she ashamed of him? Maybe she wished she could marry Plik instead with his thick chest and apparent command of the village. Too bad for her Plik already had a wife—one who had not defied her husband by coming in the first place. His parents had not come either, Zeff noted. Maybe Plik did have command of the village if he could command even their father—the village head.

"Listen here, little brother." Plik thumped his fist against Zeff's chest. "We don't just hunt for the village. We protect it from any who would do us harm. And there are more of those than you think. Sitting around listening to the singer spin his pretty lies of gods and devils weakens us. Makes us vulnerable. I'm doing what is best for everyone."

Zeff put his hands on his hips, ignoring the pain in his chest. "You shouldn't get to decide that for all of us. Father lets us choose."

Plik snorted. "And you see what Father chose today." He shoved Zeff again, this time hard enough to send him sprawling onto his bottom in the dirt. "Get back to your fishing. Have you even caught anything today?"

Zeff stood up. His limbs shook. He might have asked the hunters the same question, but he didn't. If he'd had the strength to punch Plik right in the nose, he might have done it, but that would only end with him beaten half to death. No point in it.

Plik and his hunting party moved away, laughing at him. A multitude of things he might have said ran through Zeff's brain. Too late now. He considered going after Ivy and...and what? Apologizing? Explaining himself? Asking her why she didn't stand by him? He kicked at the dirt. All things considered, he ought to just go back to fishing.

But the uneasy, irritated, ants-in-the-chest feeling would not leave him. It had started before with his strange dream. He walked away from the village, but instead of going back to the shore, he followed the footprints of the singer.

He caught up with the holy man quicker than he expected. "Excuse me, singer," he called, and the white-haired man turned around, smiling.

"Zeff. Thank you for your bravery back there. Not many will come to my defense like that."

"It didn't do any good, though," Zeff said. "I don't understand why everyone lets Plik push them around like that, even my father—our village head." Zeff rubbed the sore spot on his chest. "Just because he's bigger and stronger than the rest of us." Zeff was no weakling. He could fish and climb trees and even hunt as well as any of the other boys, but he didn't have Plik's impressive strength. No one did. It made no sense.

The singer put a hand on Zeff's shoulder. "That is often the way of it in this world," he said. "Walk with me. I think we have much to talk about."

They set off through the forest again. Wind rustled through the palm fronds overhead. Their footsteps stirred up the rich, loamy scent of the soil. Bright butterflies danced in a halo around their heads. The breeze carried the tangy scent of the sea.

"Why did you come after me?" the singer asked.

Zeff could hardly explain it to himself, just that he couldn't bear to have the songs silenced. He wanted…something, something more than what he had.

"Plik says your songs are foolish stories, but I

don't think so. Tell me, are they true?"

"They are the deepest kind of truth," the singer said, his voice solemn, weighty. "The truth of eternity. Where we came from. Where we are going. Do you believe the songs, Zeff?"

"Yes, I believe them, and when you sing them…I can see…" He paused.

"See what?" the holy man prompted.

"I can see it all," Zeff blurted before he lost the courage to speak. "The stars, the heavens, the world coming into being. It's beautiful and frightening, and everything all at once."

"I see it too. Such grandeur and majesty!" The singer looked past Zeff up in to the trees. "All of it being created and destroyed every moment. The constant balancing act of the cosmos."

Zeff shivered. He could almost feel the grand dance of the divine the holy man spoke of. It trembled through his body, through his mind, through his spirit. He thought if he closed his eyes, he could lose himself in the dance forever.

"Meet me tonight," the singer said. "On the seashore where we can see the stars. I have much to teach you."

"I will come," Zeff promised.

## V.

The dormitory where Joseph was assigned to sleep stank of urine and sweat and vomit. The too-thin blanket scratched uncomfortably against his limbs. He couldn't sleep. The metal cot didn't even have a mattress, and the snoring of a dozen other men and women wouldn't let him rest despite his weariness.

He wanted the feather mattress and the comforter his mother had made. He wanted Peggy beside him, and his hand resting against her belly, feeling the baby move inside her. He wanted his own belly full of food he'd raised himself. He squeezed his eyes shut against the threat of tears. Crying in this ugly, stinking room would surely get him beaten up or worse. Behind his closed eyes were other sights, other smells, clean and fresh. The forest and the sea. But he didn't know how to get to that place.

Judge Morris's words ran through his brain in an endless loop. They had all day as he worked in the weapons manufacturing plant. The job was simple enough—just check each gun coming off the line and make sure none of the pieces fell off. A lot of the pieces did fall off, and got tossed into a metal bin about four feet square labeled *Recycle.*

They weren't like the guns the soldiers who had come to his farm had carried. These had short, flimsy barrels and looked like they wouldn't last more than a few shots. Joseph had worked only half a day and seen thousands of the shabby weapons come off the line.

He'd asked the dark-haired girl standing next to him, "What are these for?"

"The war." She rolled her eyes like that ought to be obvious.

The trigger fell off of the next gun he picked up. "Don't seem like they'll last too long."

"Don't have to, do they?" The girl shrugged. "Soldiers on the front line don't last too long, either." She smiled an unpleasant smile, revealing browned and broken teeth. "Don't you know, white boy? You and me are just biding our time until it's our turn to get called up."

"To the front lines?"

"Yup." She nodded. "Personally, I hope it's sooner than later."

Joseph had stared down at the weapon in his hands. How could she say that? Did she want to die? Maybe she wanted to do her part, like Judge Morris had said. Do what was best for everyone. Did that really mean fighting and dying in a war?

He hadn't asked any more questions like *Where is the front line? Who are we at war with? Why?*

Now, lying in the hot and windowless dormitory, he couldn't sleep for the questions chasing around his brain. His parents wouldn't have taught him lies. He couldn't believe they had. But was it possible they were mislead like Judge Morris said Joseph was?

This place—the fortress people called it— sucked out hope like a sump pump. Nothing had any color, only gray and black, smoke and dust. His lips were coated with it. Judge Morris had told the truth about people being sick and hungry. Dinner, the only food he'd had all day, was a dry, compressed cake that tasted like dirt. The soldiers had carried away eggs and milk and cheese and fruit from his house, but that hadn't ended up in the fortress, it seemed.

And there was nothing to drink but reddish, tepid water. Or alcohol. Plenty of that around. Joseph had never drunk alcohol in his life, and he couldn't bring himself to do it today, even though he'd been laughed at for refusing. The drinks smelled worse than the water. He swallowed into his dry and scratchy throat, but it didn't help his thirst. It was easy to believe God had abandoned this place. Or didn't exist at all.

His chest ached like someone had punched it. He could no more pray in here than he could cry. So he didn't. But tears came sliding down his cheeks of their own accord. He pulled the blanket over his face to wipe them away with the rough fabric.

*What about Peggy?* That question plagued him

most of all. Where was she now? Was she okay? If he ran back to her, Judge Morris and his soldiers would surely find and execute them both. Or bring Peggy back to the fortress—that might be worse than death. No. Seeing her disillusioned like he was would kill him.

His nose started running, and he muffled his sniffing with the blanket.

"Hey, kid." A rough voice spoke to his left. Joseph held his breath and pretended not to hear.

"Yeah, you kid. The sniffler. Sit up. I wanna talk to you."

With shaking hands, Joseph pushed back the blanket and sat up. All he could see were dark blobs scattered through the room. The blob on his left was sitting up. "Yeah?" Joseph said, hoping his voice wasn't shaking as bad as the rest of him was.

"Where'd you come from? I thought all your kind were gone."

"My…my kind?"

"Blond haired, blue eyed pasty whites. Thought McKutcheon's got them all."

"Uh—no. I mean, I don't have McKutcheon's."

"No shit, or you wouldn't be here."

Joseph cringed at the bad word. And what did he mean anyway? Judge Morris had said they could cure McKutcheon's now.

"So where'd you come from?"

"I…I…I don't know."

"You retarded or something?"

Joseph didn't know what retarded was, but the man's voice implied stupid and Joseph wasn't stupid. At least he didn't think he was. "The soldiers found us."

"The judge's troopers? You're an illegal, then. I thought those were all gone, too."

Joseph toyed with the blanket. "I don't know what an illegal is."

"Geez, you really are retarded."

Joseph didn't answer that. He lay back down on the bare metal that was supposed to be a bed.

"What was it like? Where you come from?" The man's voice softened.

"Not like here." Joseph wanted to tell him about the yellow farmhouse and the little pond with the ducks and the chicken coop and the green hill where he and Peggy had buried their parents. But his throat was too tight, the tears would surely betray him, and he didn't know if this stranger might betray him too.

"You don't want to talk, kid? Fine. I was just trying to be friendly."

Nobody had tried to be friendly to him all day, except for Judge Morris. But that hadn't been a real kind of friendliness, had it? "Sorry," Joseph mumbled.

The man snorted. "Just go to sleep."

As if he could sleep. "Can you…can…can you tell me who we're at war with?"

The stranger laughed harshly. "The whole effin' world kid."

"Why?" It came out so quiet Joseph wasn't sure the man had heard it.

But after a lengthy silence, the man's gravelly voice came out of the darkness. "I don't know. That's for the higher-ups to worry about. We just gotta do our duty, right?"

"And that'll make things better?"

"So they say."

"Has it gotten better?"

"Not for a long time." He sounded sad. Weary. A lot like Joseph felt.

"Goodnight," Joseph said after a minute in barely a whisper of breath.

"Sure kid. As good as it gets, anyway."

# VI.

Zeff slipped through the forest as easily in the dark as during the day. The land spoke to him, the soil and the trees. The nocturnal beasts moved around him, all of them in a sinuous harmony with the night. He'd waited until the village was asleep, making sure no one saw him leave. It was far into the night before Plik and the rest of the hunters finished their drinking and dancing to celebrate the hunt, and finally went to bed. Zeff hoped the singer would still be waiting for him.

At last he emerged from the forest onto the moonlit sand. The singer was there, sitting cross-legged, facing the ocean with his face turned up to the moon. Zeff came up beside him. The old man's eyes were closed. He might have been asleep. Zeff touched his shoulder.

"Sit down," the singer said without opening his eyes. Zeff lowered himself onto the sand, still warm from the sun. "Close your eyes," he instructed, "and listen."

Zeff let the moonlight bathe his face, and listened to the murmur of the waves tugging on the shore, to the night noises of the forest behind him. The breeze whispered in his ear of the secrets of the endless sea. Even the moonlight hummed a gentle melody, strange and familiar at the same time. This was the music he'd heard his whole life.

"Listen deeper," the singer whispered. Zeff filled his lungs with the sea air and exhaled slowly, letting the throbbing drumbeat of his heart match the rhythm of the world. His body quivered. Scenes unfolded in his mind like before. Stars unfolding in the void like blossoming flowers. The world spinning into being, a beautiful blue-green pearl. Beings of light surrounded the pearl, cupping it in their hands. Zeff's heart sang

But not all of the song was joyful. The vision of creation faded, and from the sand and the sea and the wind through the trees, he heard another melody—a strain of sorrow, grief, and pain. He opened his eyes and looked a the singer. "Mother Earth suffers."

"Yes." The singer ran his fingers through the sand. "She mourns for the wickedness of her children."

Zeff nodded. The darkness was there in everyone, even inside his own heart, a constant struggle, just like the struggle between creation and destruction.

The singer began a new song, one Zeff had not heard before. The tale of the coming of the Son of God to save the world. To conquer the darkness and evil forever.

"When will he come?" Zeff whispered.

"Hundreds of generations from now."

"Oh."

The singer must have sensed Zeff's disappointment at that because he laid a hand on Zeff's shoulder. "But His sacrifice will transcend time. It will reach backward and forward and encompass all of us."

Zeff's skin tingled. "How?"

"That is the great mystery, isn't it? If you come with me, I can teach you much more."

"You mean—leave the village?" Zeff stared out at the waves, shimmering blackly in the moonlight. "I am betrothed."

"If your brother will not allow me in your village, you must come to me."

"For how long?"

"As long as you need." Though Zeff could not read the holy man's expression in the darkness, he could hear the earnestness in the man's voice. His heart thrummed wildly in his chest. He didn't want to leave Ivy and Fern, his parents and friends.

But the songs filled him with joy the way nothing else did—not even Ivy. Really, he didn't even know if Ivy truly loved him.

"I will come with you," he told the singer. "I want to learn from you. But I need to go home first. Talk to my family and my betrothed."

"Yes, that is wise. I can meet you here tomorrow at sunset."

"Thank you." Zeff clasped the singer's arm.

"You will not regret it, young man."

A crashing sound through the trees caught both their attention. Zeff tensed. It might be a wild boar or a hunting cat, and he'd brought no weapon. But it wasn't an animal that stumbled onto the beach. It was his brother Plik, carrying a torch in one hand and his stone hunting dagger in the other.

"What are you doing?" Plik bellowed, and from the slur in his speech and the way he staggered across the sand, Zeff guessed he was drunk.

"Nothing, Plik." He held up his hands in a placating gesture. "We were talking. That's all. You wouldn't allow him in the village."

"You're plotting against me, aren't you?" Plik swung his torch in Zeff's direction. Zeff and the singer took a step back

"No Nothing like that," Zeff said. "Plik, you aren't thinking clearly."

"You agreed to kill me, didn't you?"

"Don't be silly. You're my brother. I'd never kill you. Or anyone."

Plik advanced toward Zeff, waving his dagger. "You think you can be the next village head? Well, you can't. That's my place, got it?"

"I know." Zeff backed away from the menacing blade. "I don't want to be village head." He glanced at the singer. "I'm leaving the village. I want to learn more from the singer."

"Liar! You're both plotting to destroy me."

"Please calm down." The singer stepped up beside Zeff. "You've had too much to drink. Why don't you put down that dagger? Zeff can take you home."

Plik growled, an inhuman sound He lunged forward, dagger raised to strike.

"No!" Zeff stumbled backward until his feet hit the water, but Plik was too fast. He drove the dagger toward Zeff—

—and the singer threw himself between Zeff and Plik's deadly blade.

Plik plunged the dagger into the old man's chest. Zeff caught him as he fell, too stunned to even cry out. Blood spread over the singer's tunic. Zeff fell to his bottom under the weight of the singer's limp body. This couldn't be happening. He still had so much to learn. He pressed his hand over the wound. Blood ran slick and hot under his fingers. Plik stood over them, breathing hard. His hand still clutched the dagger, but the murder must have sobered him and cooled the fire of his drunken rage.

"Why?" Zeff cried. His voice burned through his raw throat. "Why did you kill him?"

A look of horror passed over Plik's face for a moment as he stared at the dying man. An expression so full of anguish that Zeff knew in that instant he could forgive his brother for his mistake. "Plik—" Zeff held out his hand.

But Plik's eyes hardened in a blink, so fast Zeff wondered if he'd imagined the anguish and regret of a moment before.

"This is your fault!" Plik shouted.

"What?"

"I know what you want, little brother. I know what you were planning."

"No." Zeff struggled out from under the singer's body. "You're wrong." Frustration and grief brought prickly tears to his eyes. "Please, Plik. Let's go home. We'll forget about all this."

"You aren't coming home." Plik slashed his dagger again. Zeff dodged, but the blade caught him across his upper arm. He hissed in pain and fear of the cruel madness that had seized his brother. Plik growled like an animal again.

Zeff ran, skirting sideways around Plik, and sprinted for the trees. Plik gave chase. His torch guttered, leaving them in darkness. Though Zeff was smaller and quicker, Plik's rage fueled his speed and his pounding footsteps and ragged breathing grew louder in Zeff's ears.

Zeff's heart almost burst out of his chest. Plik had his anger, but Zeff had fear for his life to drive him on. His brother wanted to kill him. That hurt worse than the pain from running so hard. Worse than the sting of the cut on his arm.

The moonlight did not penetrate the canopy of the forest. In the blind darkness, Zeff plunged between the trees. The roaring of his panic garbled and muted the voice of the forest, but still he managed to skirt around trees and other obstacles. Plik wasn't so lucky. His crashes and cursing sent the night creatures scampering for cover.

Zeff threw himself onto a tree trunk and scrambled upward with his fingers and toes like a nimble monkey, up as high as he dared go. He wrapped his arms and legs around the trunk and held his breath. Trusting in the darkness to hide him.

Plik lumbered by beneath the tree, still swearing and out of breath. Zeff stayed still. The bark prickled against his skin. Blood dripped from the slash on his arm. He didn't move even after Plik had moved deeper into the forest. His quivering muscles and the splinters in his fingers helped to dull the pain in his heart. The singer—dead. How could it be? And what was Zeff to do now? Go home and hope Plik's rage wore off by morning?

No. First he'd have to bury the singer properly. Then maybe he could go home, marry Ivy, and hope for another to come with singer's knowledge. Were there others?

Suddenly Plik's voice rang through the

darkness, nearly startling Zeff out of his tree.

"Don't you dare come back to the village, Zeff," he bellowed. "I will kill you. I will tell father and everyone what I heard you planning. He'll agree with your banishment."

*I wasn't planning anything,* Zeff screamed silently. *You couldn't have heard what was never said.*

Surely, no one would believe Plik's tale. The village knew Zeff's character and Plik's. He thought about the way everyone had left the singer without a word. Maybe they would believe Plik, or at least not dare to contradict him.

"I know you're nearby, you sneaky little snake. I know you can hear me. If I see your face again, you're a dead man."

He'd do it. He would kill Zeff to cover up his murder of the singer. He'd convince himself his drunken lies were truths.

*I can't go home.*

A drizzle of rain dripped through the treetops. Zeff shimmied down the tree. He didn't even care if Plik was waiting for him at the bottom. His chest felt heavy as a stone. How could everything have fallen apart so quickly? He collapsed as his feet touched the ground, and the rain drizzled forlornly on his shuddering form, washing away the blood running down his arm.

## VII.

Joseph stumbled a little, the ache in his chest was so exquisite. The man stabbed and bleeding on the seashore. The panicked flight into the forest. For a moment those visions had seemed more real than the weapons factory. The bits and pieces of this other life left an echo in his heart.

"Stop daydreaming," the man beside him snarled, and shoved him away. Joseph dropped the gun he was holding. It broke in pieces against the concrete floor.

"Clean that up," the man snapped. It wasn't the man who'd spoken to him that first night. At least, he didn't think so. The man in the dorm hadn't spoken to him again. Joseph bent to retrieve the broken gun. Someone—he thought it was the angry man, but he couldn't be sure—shoved him to the ground. His shoulder slammed hard into the concrete.

"Oh, for Pete's sake." The woman to his other side aimed a kick at his back. "You're completely useless. Get out of here."

Joseph winced and grunted coming to his feet. The angry man and the woman had closed the gap he'd left in the line, and when he tried to work his way back in, the woman swung her elbow at his chest. His hands curled into fists, but what was he going to do? Punch somebody over his place in a crappy weapons factory that smelled of grease and sweat and smoke?

Instead, he ground his teeth together and stomped outside. The air was not any better out here. It stung his eyes and made him cough. It hadn't been that bad this morning when he'd tromped with the others from the dormitory to the factory. Smoke and ash must have blown in from some distant battlefield. The front lines, wherever that was. He hadn't seen the girl he'd talked to since that first day. Maybe she'd gotten her wish to go to the front lines. Of course, her wish meant death.

A tremor passed through Joseph. Would death be any worse than this? The thought made his empty stomach churn. He had always believed at death he would be with his parents again, that someday he and Peggy and all their children would be together in heaven. But Peggy was gone—alone somewhere if she wasn't dead herself—and his parents' promises of safety and peace were shattered.

He looked down at his hands. They'd always seemed so strong to him, able to take care of the farm and Peggy. He'd dreamed of holding his own newborn baby in those hands. But now they were gray and sunken. Weak. He was hungry and exhausted. Everything he'd ever cared about was gone. *I hope it's sooner than later,* the girl had said. Now Joseph understood just what she meant.

He fell to his knees, head in his hands, part of him wanted to pray, but the words wouldn't come.

"What are you doing?"

Joseph jerked his head up. One of the soldiers—Judge Morris's troopers—stood above him with his rifle pointed straight at Joseph's heart. "I...uh..."

"On your feet," the trooper barked. Joseph jumped up, heart racing. "You should be at your assigned work station."

"I know. I just...I ..." He swallowed. "They don't want me there."

The trooper made a rude noise in his throat. "Better go ask for reassignment, then."

"Will I be sent to the front lines?"

There was no reading the trooper's face behind his helmet, but Joseph imagined him sneering.

"Not my call," the trooper said. "Just go before I have to lock you up for not working."

Joseph nodded, moving away toward the tall glass and steel building Judge Morris had taken him to weeks ago. He'd seen no sign of the judge since then. His threats still rang loud in Joseph's ears. Maybe his troopers had gone back to the farm. Maybe they'd found Peggy and killed her because Joseph had lied. How would he even know?

He looked over his shoulder. The trooper had moved on. This could be his chance. No one else was around. If he didn't get reassigned anywhere, maybe he could escape and no one would know he was gone. He could find Peggy and they could hide somewhere new and start over. He took a few more steps toward the tall building. So many questions ran through his mind.

Could he get through the thick wall with its barbed wire top? Could he find his way back to the farm? Would he even find Peggy there? Was there any way to survive?

And there were other questions—the questions he didn't want to ask himself anymore.

It would never work. Peggy was lost to him, lost forever. A fierce longing seized him. A longing to return to his life before the troopers had come, when he and Peggy were the only two people in the world. When he hadn't been hungry and afraid. When he hadn't been filled with doubt. But that was a childish desire, to want to turn his back on reality. Ignore the suffering of the rest of the world.

Judge Morris had accused his parents of doing just that, and he was right. They had turned their backs on the world, and created a haven where their child could live in light and peace. What would become of Joseph's child?

He took two or three more faltering steps toward the skyscraper—toward reassignment and duty and despair. Then he turned and ran toward the outer wall of the fortress. He would get through it or he would get over it somehow. There had to be a way.

Shouts sounded all around him. Maybe the troopers would shoot him. He didn't care. He'd be out of the fortress one way or another. He concentrated on pushing himself faster on his weakened, weary legs. On running like that other boy had—Zeff—when he ran from his brother.

A shrill scream louder than anything Joseph had ever heard brought him to a startled halt. A fireball the size of his farmhouse split the sky overhead, and Joseph realized the shouts had not been about him at all.

The fortress was under attack.

Joseph and his fellow workers had drilled for such an event twice a week, but the shriek of the fiery projectile put all that training out of his head.

The bomb hit with a noise so deafening it was more like a sudden, complete silence, and the world blazed white. Joseph fell, and seemed to fall forever without hitting the ground. Sight and sound both were swallowed up in the unending brilliant white, and he wondered if he had died.

His body met the ground with a painful crunch. The white faded to ordinary daylight. Rocks and dirt and steel and glass and chunks of concrete rained down around him. He tried to cover his head with his arms, but nothing could protect him from the onslaught. He squeezed his eyes shut and waited for it to end—if it would ever end. A wailing filled his ears with sound again, and he realized he was hearing some kind of alarm or warning siren.

The warning had come too late.

Joseph climbed to his feet, shaking all over. Cuts on his face and hands bled and stung, and his body ached, but he didn't seem seriously injured. Ash and dust continued to rain from a sky darkened with smoke. The larger pieces of debris had—he hoped—all come down now.

The skyscraper that had dominated the fortress was…gone. Noting remained but some pieces of foundation, and those were burning. Joseph turned in a circle. Everything was burning. The movement made his head swim. He stumbled to his knees and pushed himself up again. The world spun. Flames greedily licked the walls of the factories and dorms.

The wailing alarm cut off abruptly and left his ears ringing. Joseph put a hand to his head and tried to take a step forward. It didn't work. He fell onto his hands and knees and vomited bile from his empty stomach. Smoke from the fires burned his throat worse than the bile. A cough shuddered through his lungs. He still couldn't stand, so he crawled in whatever direction took him away from the fires.

More explosions echoed around him. He thought they came from the direction of the ruined city. His eyes watered so much he could hardly see. His hands scraped over rubble, pierced by sharp bits of debris, but the worst was when he encountered the soft flesh of a dead body, and he had to clench his teeth to keep from vomiting again.

He saw no one alive.

For an eternity he crawled through the hellish landscape, coughing and choking and wondering if he ought to just give up, lie down among the ashes, and wait for death. But he kept going. Something drove him on. Maybe it was his longing for Peggy or his memories of the farm. Or maybe a spark of hope remained in there. A tiny seed of faith.

Whatever it was, Joseph pressed forward until breathing became easier. His eyes didn't sting so much. The ground, while not soft, was less of an agony on his hands.

He stopped with his head bent for a few shaky breaths. Then, slowly, he lifted his gaze. Sunset glowed a fierce orange and red. The scent of smoke still lingered. He came to his feet, swaying a little, but the ringing in his ears had faded and he could stand without falling. He faced the sunset and didn't turn around. If anyone was coming after him, he didn't want to know it.

His sore hands curled into fists of determination. He didn't know where he was exactly, but he would find his way back to Peggy, in hopes that she was still alive.

His first few steps wobbled, but he stayed upright. He didn't think he could crawl anymore with how much his hands and knees hurt, and hunger and fear left him weak.

The sunset darkened into a smoky dusk. Joseph wandered through a pathless maze of ruined homes overgrown with morning glory and thistle. Stunted saplings poked their heads up here and there among the weeds. What had this place looked like before it was destroyed and abandoned? In the fading light, the place felt haunted. The ghosts of once-happy families lurked behind ruined walls and burnt trees. Joseph felt hardly more substantial than these specters of his imagination.

The stars came out, dimmed by the endless pall of smoke, and eventually Joseph left behind the remains of the houses. The sound of running water caught his ear, and he broke into a limping jog toward the noise.

The little creek burbled through a stand of trees. In the moonlight, it was the most beautiful sight he'd ever seen. He collapsed to his knees, scooping the cold, precious liquid into his mouth and down his parched throat.

The water held a slight metallic tang, but he didn't care. He sucked it down greedily, without restraint, until his belly protested, then flopped onto his back with his head on the shore and his body immersed in the cooling stream, and fell into a dreamless sleep.

# VIII.

Zeff stood when the morning sunlight filtered down through the leaves. The memory of fire, smoke, ashes, and death left him trembling. The pale boy had been there, thin and hungry, hollow as a dead tree. Why did Zeff continue to see him? What could it mean?

Maybe the singer could have answered those questions. Zeff rubbed his arms and winced when his fingers met the cruel cut Plik had given him. It wasn't bleeding anymore, but he'd need some healing plants to stop the rot. That was easy enough to get in the village, but he couldn't go back there. His heart sank within him. Plik's anger might cool, but he was too proud and stubborn to ever admit he was wrong—to admit that he'd murdered the singer in a fit of rage.

Grief swelled in his chest. He had to go back to the beach and lay the singer to rest properly. What came after that—well, he didn't want to think about it right now.

He plodded back through the trees he had practically flown through last night. He couldn't make his feet go any faster. Too soon he emerged onto the sand. The singer was there, his body stretched out on the sand. The tide had gone out, leaving him several feet away from the edge of the water.

And he wasn't alone. A girl knelt beside the singer, her face buried in her hand. Zeff hesitated. Who could she be? Did the singer have family? Other students? If so, he ought to leave the burial to them. Zeff was nearly a stranger after all.

But the girl was too slight to lift the singer's body herself, and no one else was around. At the very least, he should offer his help and condolences. With a lump in his throat, he approached the weeping girl. Most of the blood had washed away with the tide, but the hole in the singer's chest gaped like an angry demonic mouth. Zeff shuddered. Gently, he touched the girl on the shoulder.

She jumped back from his touch and came to her feet with a slender obsidian knife in her hands. Zeff took a step back, raising his hands.

"Who are you?" the girl demanded. "Did you kill you my father?"

"No." He shook his head vigorously. "He was my friend."

The girl studied him through narrowed eyes. At last, she tucked the knife into the belt tied around the waist of her dress. "Do you know what happened? Who killed him?" Fresh tears gathered in her eyes.

"Yes." Zeff looked at his feet. "I came to talk to the—to your father. I wanted to learn more from him, but my brother had forbid him to come to our village. Plik, my brother, he had too much to drink. He followed me here. He said I was plotting to kill him. He wasn't in his right mind. When he tried to stab me, your father…he saved my life."

The girl covered her mouth with her hand, and the tears flowed down her cheeks. Zeff wanted to touch her to comfort her somehow, but he didn't even know her, and she still carried the knife. Her pain pierced him. It was his fault in a way. If he'd just let the singer go home, none of this would have happened. The singer would still be alive and Zeff would still be welcome in the village.

"I'm so, so sorry," he whispered, blinking back tears of his own. "I will help you bury him if you want me to."

The girl nodded. She wiped the tears from her cheeks. "Thank you."

"What's your name?" Zeff asked.

She sniffed. "It's Dahlia."

"I'm Zeff."

Dahlia dipped her head in acknowledgement. Her eyes went back to her father's body, and her shoulders slumped.

"We will have to take him back to your village."

Dahlia shook her head. "We have no village. Wait here. Our camp is not far away. I will come back with everything we need." She closed her eyes and pressed her hand to her chest for a moment.

Then she looked at Zeff again. "Will you stay with him until I return?"

"Yes." Zeff watched her disappear into the trees with the grace and subtlety of a young deer. He lowered himself onto the sand beside the singer. The body had already grown stiff and cold. The pain in Zeff's chest increased.

So, the singer and his daughter had no village to belong to. That surprised him. How did one survive without a village? He rested his hands on his thighs, closed his eyes, and quietly sang the singer's song of creation. But the words stuck in his throat, and the melody dissolved into the crashing of the waves.

Dahlia came back a short time later with a skin bag over her shoulder, stuffed so full she bent beneath its weight.

Zeff came to her and took the heavy burden.

"Thank you." She rested her hands on her knees and tried to catch her breath. Zeff set the bag beside the body and peered in at the contents. Clothing, jars of herbs and ointments, tools, and other items he didn't know the uses of. He had a million questions for her, but he kept them back while they prepared the body.

With some difficulty, they removed the singer's bloodstained clothes. Dahlia had herbs, flowers, and ointments for every part of the body. Zeff watched mostly in silence, and handed Dahlia whatever she asked for. He found it fascinating, much more intricate than any burial preparation he'd seen in the village.

She sang as she anointed him, but Zeff did not understand the words. The melody was poignant and pressed on his heart. When she finished, Zeff helped her to dress him in soft, white clothing, different from anything he'd seen before. Dahlia treated the clothing with the utmost care, brushing off any sand and arranging it all just so. Satisfied it was all on properly, she placed a belt of green, woven leaves on his waist, and a necklace of pink and purple flowers around his neck. Then she bent and kissed his forehead and whispered something in his ear.

"He's ready." Dahlia stood and brushed the sand from her dress. Her chin quivered. Zeff risked another hand to her shoulder. This time she didn't move away or pull her knife. She gave him a sad, half-smile and looked down at her father again.

"I can dig the grave," Zeff said as gently as possible. "Just tell me where."

Dahlia chose a pretty spot beneath a tall grandmother of a tree whose branches hung low and swayed in the breeze. Wildflowers of yellow and purple grew all around the trunk, and ivy twined up around it.

Zeff set to work with a stout digging stick

Dahlia had brought in her bag. It took hours, but he enjoyed having something to do to take his mind off of everything else. When the hole was big enough, he returned to the beach where Dahlia kept vigil beside the singer.

Zeff's heart grew heavy as he gathered the body into his arms and carried it into the forest with Dahlia trailing behind, softly weeping. He laid the singer down carefully in his grave, straightening the strange funeral clothing and the flower necklace. Dahlia nodded her approval, so he stood and began to shovel the dirt back into the hole over the singer's body. Dahlia sang as he did so, in a high, clear voice as sweet as a songbird greeting the dawn. It was a song of mourning, yes, but it was also a song of joy. A song to welcome a son of God back home. A song that ignited visions in Zeff's mind—visions of light and glory. By the time the song ended, he'd finished filling in the grave, and he and Dahlia gathered wildflowers to pile atop the fresh mound. At last, they stood in silence with heads bowed.

"Your father said he'd teach me about his songs—about the Son of God. He asked me to leave my village and come with him, and I would have..." he trailed off.

Dahlia gave him a sharp look. "He did?" Her cheeks flushed.

"Yes."

Again her eyes studied his face, sizing him up. "That is not an offer my father would make lightly. He must have thought highly of you." She turned her face away.

"I don't know," Zeff said. "I did think highly of him."

"So did I." A shudder passed through her.

"Do you have anywhere to go? Any other family?" Zeff asked.

Dahlia shook her head. "It was just my father and me, but we always knew this was a possibility." She indicated the flower-covered grave. "Men like him, who speak the truth, tend to make enemies." She faltered, but recovered herself quickly enough. "So I am prepared to live on my own." She lifted her chin, as if to look brave, but Zeff saw it quiver. Alone was no way to live. His stomach felt all hollowed out and twisted around itself.

"My brother forbid me to come home. He said he'd kill me if I did, and I believe him." Plik's face flashed through his mind. The anguish on it when he realized he'd killed the singer. Zeff knew in his heart that Plik would do anything—even commit another murder—to justify that action to himself. "So, I guess I'm on my own too." He shrugged.

"Except you have nothing," Dahlia said. She clucked her tongue sadly.

"Yes." Zeff looked down at his feet. He wasn't

sure what he was getting at exactly. He had planned to stay with the singer, but now he didn't know what to do.

Dahlia laid her hand on his arm. "Surely your brother wouldn't kill you in cold blood. You should go home."

"He killed your father," Zeff pointed out and immediately wished he hadn't. "But—I don't think he meant to do that. He was drunken and not in his right mind." Zeff wrapped his arms around himself. "I think…he wouldn't want to see me. I'd remind him of the awful thing he did."

"But what about your family? Your mother and father? Or do you have a wife?" She turned pink again.

"No, but I am betrothed. Or I was yesterday. I don't know if Ivy still wants me. She…admires Plik a great deal." He chest felt funny and tight. He'd been willing to give up Ivy and everything to follow the singer. Nothing was certain anymore.

"Then you must go home," Dahlia said firmly. "You owe it to her. To your family. They wouldn't want you to disappear."

She was right. Even if they believed Plik—or didn't dare defy him—his family and Ivy would want to see him and know what had happened. At least, he hoped they would.

But even if Plik let him come home, even if he

was welcomed back with open arms and married Ivy and lived in peace the rest of his days, he would still long for the knowledge the singer had been willing to teach him.

"Dahlia, do you know anyone else like your father? A singer who could teach me?" Maybe it was selfish to ask as they stood over her father's grave, but if she left and he never saw her again—he had to know.

She shook her head, blinking back tears.

"Could you teach me?"

"No. Not me." She spun away from him, running back toward the beach.

"Wait," Zeff called after her. "Dahlia, stop. I'm sorry." He jogged behind her until he could catch hold of her elbow. "Please stop. I shouldn't have asked. Forgive me. It's just…so important to me, you know?"

She covered her face with her hands and wept. "Yes. Yes, I know." Her sobs muffled the words.

Zeff stood helpless in the face of her grief. He wished he dared put his arms around her and console her as he would Fern or his other sisters, but he didn't. Still, he couldn't leave her alone like this.

"Come with me."

She shook her head.

"You shouldn't be alone. We can watch and wait until my brother is gone. He leaves often to hunt. Please. My family owes you something for your father's death. Come. Let my mother take care of you for a while."

Dahlia lifted her head with confusion in her eyes. "She would do that?"

"Yes, she would. And my little sister, Fern. You'll love her." The tightness returned to his chest. "I may have to leave, but you haven't wronged anyone. You could stay in the village as long as you need."

"But your brother," she protested. "How could I stay with him there?"

"I don't know. Maybe you couldn't. Maybe we'll only have a few days or a few hours. But—it doesn't seem right to leave you here alone. Maybe my village can offer you something, even if only for a short time." He held his breath, waiting for her response.

Dahlia blinked away her hears. "Thank you. You are very kind. I will come."

Zeff let out his breath. A great weight lifted off him, though he didn't know for certain if either of them would be welcomed in the village. He had done the right thing. He was sure of it.

# IX.

"Go home," Joseph whispered. The thought of it spilled warmth into his chest despite the cold seeping through the rest of his body.

"Wake up!" Rough hands shook him. "What are you doing in there? Wake up!"

Joseph's eyes popped open. A white-haired, white-bearded face leered into his. The man shook him again. Joseph groaned. He hurt from tip to toe, but his stomach ached the most. He clutched is middle and bent forward, groaning again.

"Drank the water, did ya?" The old man shook his head. "What'd you do that for? Don't you know it's poisoned?"

Poisoned? How would he know that? "Am I…am I going to die?" As much as he hurt, he thought death might be a welcome relief, but now he needed to find Peggy.

"Get up." The man hauled him out of the stream by one arm. "I got to ya in time, I think. You come with me, and I'll get you fixed up."

Joseph winced, coming to his feet. Isn't that just what Judge Morris had said to him? The old man slid his arm under Joseph's and helped him stand and walk. His wet clothes chafed against his skin, and he prayed he wouldn't have to go too far. His body didn't seem strong enough to take a step.

"Where'd you come from, anyway?" the old man asked. Don't get many folk wandering through my woods these days. 'Specially not folk like you."

*Blond-haired, blue-eyed pasty whites?* The man had sun-browned, leathery skin beneath his wild hair and beard, and his eyes looked strikingly familiar. Joseph stopped, stumbling, as he realized why. "Judge Morris?"

The old man grunted. "Come from the fortress, did ya?"

"Yes. Well, no. I mean…" His stomach clenched and pain shuddered through his body.

The old man who looked like the judge gripped him tighter under his shoulders. "All right. Never mind that now. Let's get you home."

The man's home was a snug little log cabin thankfully not far from the stream. He set Joseph down on a pile of furs in one corner of the small cabin, then busied himself making tea. At least, that's what Joseph though he was doing.

The cabin consisted of one small room with a loft covering half the space. Joseph lay under the loft near the wooden ladder leading up to it. The space was close and stuffy, smelling of wood smoke and meat. Animal skins and trophy antlers cluttered the little room. Joseph had done his fair share of hunting and trapping, but this man seemed to use it as his primary means of survival.

After a few minutes, he brought Joseph a chipped ceramic mug full of foul-smelling tea. "Drink it."

"Joseph took a sip and gagged. "It's awful."

"Well, that's the point, isn't it? Gotta get the toxins out somehow." He chuckled. "Bottom's up."

Joseph wrinkled up his face and sucked down as much as he could in one gulp. His eyes widened. The old man thrust a rusted bucket into his hands, and Joseph vomited into it until he thought his whole insides had come out, and he leaned over the bucket, panting.

"Done?" the old man asked. "That'll help." He pulled the bucket out of Joseph's grip and offered him a glass of water. "This has been filtered. No danger to ya."

Joseph took a tentative sip. His stomach didn't protest, so he took another, then leaned back against the pile of furs, exhausted. The old man took the puke bucket outside, and returned a few minutes later.

He crouched in front of Joseph and offered him another mug, this one more fragrant. "This will help, too," he said, and the kindness in his voice reminded Joseph uncomfortably of the judge, too.

"Who are you?" he asked, taking the mug. "You look like Judge Morris."

"Well, I should. I'm his brother. His twin as a

matter of fact."

Joseph choked on his sip of tea. "His twin?"

"Yep. I suppose that's why he lets me live out here in peace." He sat back on his heels. "Don't look so surprised. Not everyone agrees with my brother's plan for making society better."

Joseph nodded. "My parents didn't. But Judge Morris said they were wrong. That they were selfish to do so."

"He says a lot of things, don't he? Don't make 'em true."

Joseph chewed on that for a moment, sipping his tea. How could you know what was true with so many different people saying so many different things? He missed the simplicity of his parents' teachings and the stories in the scriptures. The image of his father's Bible crumbling to ashes rose up in his mind.

"So, I take it you didn't grow up in the fortress, huh?"

"No, I didn't." Joseph closed his eyes He didn't want to go over it all again, and he wasn't sure if he could trust this man anyway. Judge Morris's twin brother?

Mr. Morris respected his silence, though, and didn't push the issue any further. "You're all cut up," he said.

Joseph touched his cheek. The cuts and bruises

stung beneath his fingers. "The fortress was attacked. Destroyed." He opened his eyes. "Oh, I'm sorry. I think your brother is dead."

"Dead?" Mr. Morris stood, glancing around the cabin as if he'd lost something. He moved to the small window. "I heard the explosions. Thought they were closer than before, but…" He leaned heavily on the glass pane. "For all his faults, the old judge and his fortress at least kept us safe here."

Safe because of a stream of disposable soldiers with disposable weapons at the front line. Joseph shuddered. Maybe this was the front line now. "I'm so sorry for your loss," Joseph said.

Mr. Morris shook his head. "It's weird, you know? I haven't seen or talked to my brother in almost twenty years, but to think that he's gone." He heaved a sigh. "Sometimes I wish our lives could have been different."

Joseph pulled his knees up to his chest, unsure what to say. It was the same way the other boy—Zeff—had felt with the singer's daughter. And maybe Zeff felt what Mr. Morris did, too. Regret over the feud with his brother. Strange how this other life seemed so close to his own.

"You got any brothers?" Mr. Morris asked gruffly, turning away from the window.

"No," Joseph said. He still didn't mention Peggy.

"Just as well," Mr. Morris grumbled. "If the fortress is gone, it's over for us. The enemy will come through here soon enough, and they don't take any prisoners."

"Who…who…who are these enemies?"

"Hell if I know. Seemed like the whole damn world was set to bring down the U.S. of A. Don't really matter who they are, does it? Only that they're coming to kill us."

Fear tingled along Joseph's nerves. "Do you believe in God?" he blurted out.

Mr. Morris turned away from the window. "Well, now, that's a question and a half, ain't it?"

"The judge—your brother—he said believing in God was foolish and led to cruelty and division, but…is that true?"

Mr. Morris came to sit beside him. "Maybe that's true in some ways. I certainly heard God's name invoked in some rotten acts in my life. But there was goodness too, and love, and miracles. Lots of cause to believe there's someone watching over us. I haven't given God any thought for a long time." He shrugged. "Maybe you and I are going to find out sooner than we think."

"You really think so? That our enemies will destroy us?"

"I'm afraid so." He put his arm around Joseph in a gesture that reminded Joseph so much of his own father that tears gathered in his eyes.

"My brother and his soldiers were the only thing standing between us and them." His eyes grew far away. "Time was I thought nothing could bring down this great country." He sagged, looking suddenly much older. "But I was wrong, wasn't I? So many of us were wrong. Maybe all of us were wrong together." He patted Joseph's shoulder. "Well, if we're gonna go down, might as well go down fighting, right?" He stood up, an odd sort of excitement about him. "Take out as many of them as we can before they get us." He rubbed his hands together.

Joseph felt queasy at the though of killing someone, even someone trying to kill him. A chill ran through him. He stood up beside Mr. Morris, and made a decision. "I have to find Peggy."

"Peggy?" Mr. Morris arched an eyebrow.

"My wife." He swallowed. "She's going to have a baby."

"Baby, huh? Hell of a time to bring a child into the world."

Joseph didn't answer, just stared at the floor, his heart pinched tight. Chances were he'd never see Peggy or the baby again.

"Was she with you at the fortress?" Mr. Morris asked, his voice softer.

Joseph shook his head. "We…we had…a farm.

In the mountains. My parents built it. The judges troopers—they didn't find Peggy. I hope they didn't find Peggy."

Mr. Morris swore under his breath, and a crushing hopelessness settled in Joseph's chest. "I won't find her in time, will I? I don't even know where our farm is."

Mr. Morris was silent for a moment. "Well, look here," he said at last, "I have some maps of the area. Maybe we can figure it out, maybe we can get there before the enemy—they may think there's nothing beyond the fortress anyway. If we're lucky, maybe we'll find your wife." He clapped Joseph on the shoulder again.

"You'll come with me?"

Mr. Morris shrugged. "Got nothin' keepin' me here. Not with the enemy coming. Let's go find the maps."

## X.

Zeff and Dahlia hid in the shadow of the trees and waited silently for Fern to pass by. It was odd to be afraid to enter his own village. They'd been waiting since before the sunrise, and Zeff was beginning to wonder if Fern was coming by here today at all. Beside him, Dahlia chewed on her fingernails and shifted restlessly.

"Shh." He held up his hand. "Someone's coming."

"Finally."

Fern came into view, carrying her collecting basket down her favorite path, but she lacked her usual, cheerful expression. Her brow furrowed, and she kept her eyes down.

"Fern," Zeff whispered. He stepped out from behind the tree.

Fern squeaked and dropped her basket. "Zeff! Oh, Zeff." She flung herself into his arms. "Where were you? I thought you were dead."

Zeff grunted in the tightness of her embrace. "I'm sorry, Fern. I'm well. I'm not dead." He gently extricated himself from her arms. "Is Plik in the village?"

"No." She put her hand to her mouth. "Is he not with you? When neither of you returned we thought you were together—in life or death." She threw her arms around his waist again. "But you're here.

You're alive. Thank the gods."

"Just one God to thank," Dahlia said quietly.

Fern stepped back, surprised.

"Fern, this is Dahlia. She is the singer's daughter."

Fern gave Zeff a questioning look.

"Let's go home. I'll tell everyone what happened."

Fern slipped her hand into his. "Do you know where Plik is?"

"No." He squeezed her hand. "No more questions until I've told my story, agreed?"

"Agreed. I'm so glad you're not dead, Zeff."

"As am I."

Fern looked over at Dahlia. "Where is your father?"

"Hush," Zeff scolded with an apologetic glance at Dahlia. "No more questions. You'll hear all I have to say soon enough."

A few minutes later, they arrived at the village. Almost at once, a crowd surrounded them. Everyone, it seemed, wanted to touch Zeff, take his hand, or pat his back. His gratitude at the warm reception nearly brought tears to his eyes. Dahlia was also welcomed kindly, though she mostly kept silent, swept along with the enthusiasm of the villagers. Someone handed her a bowl of stew, and she muttered a shy thanks.

Zeff's mother pushed her way through the rest and enfolded him in her arms. "You should not worry your mother like that."

"I'm sorry." He stepped out of her embrace. "Where is Father? I must speak to him."

"In the council hut." His mother nodded toward it, and her expression darkened a little.

"Mother, this is Dahlia. She is the daughter of the singer, and...she's lost her father."

His mother gasped. "Oh, my. I am sorry. Come with me." She put her arm around Dahlia and drew her away toward her own hut, as Zeff had hoped she would.

He caught sight of Ivy with her hand on her hip and a peevish frown on her face. He motioned for her to come to him, but she walked away with her chin in the air. Zeff didn't know if he felt more regret or relief at her anger. He'd been prepared to leave the village after all, with or without Ivy.

"Zeff, you have returned." His father's stern voice drew his attention away from Ivy.

"Father." He started forward, heart pounding with the dread of the tale he had to tell. But his steps stopped abruptly when Plik came out of the council hut behind his father, his arms folded across his massive chest. Zeff's mouth went dry.

"Plik!" Fern cried, hurrying toward her brother. She stopped, too, though when Plik did not acknowledge her presence, but kept his cold glare fixed on Zeff.

"You dared to come back?" Plik growled.

"I didn't know you were here."

"So, you hoped you could spread your lies before Father could hear the truth?"

"No." Zeff stepped out beyond the other villagers to confront Plik and his father, trying to act braver than he felt. "I came to tell him the truth."

"You came to confess your crime in plotting against me?" Plik asked, glowering.

"I was not plotting. Father, may we speak in private?"

"Whatever you have to say for yourself may be said in front of all of us," his father said, and Zeff knew he'd already made up his mind—believed whatever Plik had told him just as Plik had said he would.

"I went to speak to the singer. I wanted him to teach me his songs and stories. To teach me the truth. If Plik overheard something, he misunderstood. He was drunken."

"A lie," Plik said through his teeth.

"Plik." Zeff stepped forward, his hands outstretched. "I know it was an accident. I know you didn't mean to kill the singer. I know you didn't want to kill me. It was the wine."

"You see, Father?" Plik said. "He tires to blame

me for his own crime."

"I've done no crime," Zeff said. "Father—"

His father held up a hand to silence him. "Enough. I have seen your jealousy toward your brother. You conspired to murder him, then murdered the singer when he tried to warn your brother. That's the truth, isn't it?"

"No. No, of course not. How could you believe that?"

"You're wrong!" Fern rushed to Zeff's side and slid her hand into his. "Zeff would never murder."

"Are you implying that I would murder, little sister?" Plik asked.

Fern quailed at the tone of his voice. "No. But, maybe—" She glanced at Zeff. "Maybe it was an accident as Zeff said."

"Yes, it was an accident, Father. A misunderstanding. Please. Plik was drunken."

"I am no drunkard!"

"Yes, but that night—"

"Enough!" Their father, the headman, stood between his sons. My decision is made. Zeff you are guilty of conspiring and murder. For that you pay with your life at dawn tomorrow."

"Father, no," Zeff said, almost in a whisper. How could he even consider that? Why did Plik hate him so much? Why did his father too? A part of him was aware that his mother was pushing her way back through the crowd, throwing herself at his father's feet, pleading for his life. That Fern had wrapped herself around his legs, sobbing. That Dahlia stood apart, staring with her eyes wide, her mouth hanging open.

But as for himself, an odd detachment had come over him. He felt like an outsider, watching the scene play out without being involved. Just like the way he caught glimpses of the pale boy in the ruined world. Zeff could picture him now, in fact, moving noisily through the forest of strange trees with an old man, both of them fearful. He was searching for his wife, Zeff knew—though he didn't know how he knew it—hoping to at least see her again before the end.

*The end.* Zeff blinked back into his own reality. He wouldn't even get to have a wife before his end. He looked around for Ivy, but didn't see her. Someone grabbed his arms from behind and dragged him away.

Fern and his mother sobbed and wailed, but the rest of the village had fallen into an uncomfortable silence. No one from the village had been executed in Zeff's memory, and not for many years before that either. They were peaceful people. Murder and execution had not touched them, not that Zeff knew of. He caught his father's eyes, silently pleading for his mercy, but his father turned away, back toward the council hut. Plik followed, but not before sending Zeff a triumphant sneer.

But the last thing he saw before he was dragged out of the village and into the trees, was Dahlia watching him. Their eyes locked for just a moment before she turned away and ran.

# XI.

"Here's the old road," Mr. Morris said, pointing to the tracks of deep tire treads crushing the vegetation that had grown up over the old asphalt. Tracks left by the giant trucks of Judge Morris and his troopers. A wave of fear washed through Joseph at the memory.

The road wound its way up the mountainside, a clear path to follow. Mr. Morris's rifle shook in Joseph's hands. What would they find when they followed it? A pall of smoke tainted the sky. The trees and plants around them curled and wilted. More than once, Joseph spotted the bloated corpse of a squirrel or a rabbit among the trees. He shuddered in fear of finding Peggy like that.

Thoughts of his own death weighed heavy on him. Would he see his parents again? Peggy? Was there anything waiting on the other side of death or was it all a lie as Judge Morris had said. The world was dying around him, and maybe it didn't really matter at all, but the not knowing roiled in his stomach like spoiled milk.

"You see any soldiers, you shoot 'em, got it?"

"O-okay," Joseph muttered. He'd hunted enough to know he was a decent shot, but to kill another person? He wasn't sure he could do that. Well, maybe to save Peggy.

An enemy fighter roared low over their heads

and sent them diving for cover. "Did...did...did they see us?" Joseph whispered.

"Don't know, " Mr. Morris answered. "They mighta."

The fighters had been passing overhead all day as they hiked to the old road, but none had passed so close. For a few, tense minutes they lay flat in the brush, straining for the sounds of pursuit.

Just as Mr. Morris nodded, and Joseph started to stand, the thunder of the fighter crashed above them again, and great gouts of earth exploded around them, uprooting trees and tossing boulders.

The forest ignited around him. Burning debris fell from the sky. It was worse even than when the fortress was hit, because he was right in the middle of the flames this time. He couldn't even see Mr. Morris. The heat seared his skin even without the flames touching him. He stood. Pain lanced through his arm, and he realized it was bleeding. Hard. Flames surrounded him. Off to his right, he caught sight of Mr. Morris's body consuming in the flames. A sob escaped Joseph's throat. *I don't want to die. I want to see Peggy again. I want to live. Please.* He wasn't sure if he was praying or not The fire closed around him. He had to get away. Joseph closed his eyes, and plunged into the flames.

# XII.

It was Liv, one of Plik's hunting party, who tied Zeff's hands behind him around the trunk of a tree, then bound his feet to the tree as well. The ropes cut into his wrists and ankles, and the awkward position left him exhausted. One of Plik's friends stood guard over him at all times to prevent his escape.

Zeff pleaded with each man who came to guard him—men he'd known all his life. "Please. Let me go. You know this is unjust. I have done nothing wrong. I don't want to kill Plik. I don't want to be the headman. I just want to live in peace. Please. You must know this is true. Let me go, and I'll leave. I'll never come back."

But none of them would respond or even look at him. How was it that Plik had gotten such a strong hold over the village?

Darkness came, and Zeff gave up his pleading. He could no longer feel his arms, and breathing became difficult. Insects crawled over his bare legs and arms, and bites he could not scratch itched him monstrously. His parched throat stung whenever he tried to swallow, and hunger left his insides hollow.

Was this to be his method of death? Tied to a tree and eaten alive by bugs until he starved? No. His father had said it would happen at dawn.

Who would do it? Plik or his father or someone

else? Maybe one of the hunting party. Would the whole village come to see him die? He closed his eyes, and tears ran down his cheeks. He didn't want to die.

His thoughts turned to the singer and his stories. Was any of it true? It seemed he would never know. And what would happen after he died? Would he go on as part of the stars? He wasn't ready to find out. Not yet.

A quiet rain dripped down and wet his hair. He closed his eyes and clenched his teeth, and waited for morning—and death—to come.

# XIII.

Little by little Joseph became aware that the fire was gone and the pain was gone. He lay somewhere dark and perfectly still. A breeze ruffled his hair. Slowly he opened his eyes to see a sky bedazzled with stars.

Zeff felt life returning to his limbs. He couldn't tell exactly where he was. Not tied to a tree anymore. When had that happened? He pushed himself upright and stared up at the night sky unobstructed by the forest—the way it looked out on the beach, except these weren't his stars. "Where am I?"

Startled, Joseph sat up and saw the young man beside him. "It's you." He reached out his hand to touch him and see if he were real, but stopped just short.

Zeff stared at the pale hand frozen inches from his face. He reached up and took hold of it. "You're real." He could hardly believe it. "Where are we?" He let the pale boy—Joseph's hand drop. "Are we dead?"

*I should be dead,* Joseph thought, remembering the explosion, the flames, Mr. Morris. And Zeff had been awaiting execution, hadn't he? Maybe they were dead. He shrugged helplessly.

Zeff stood up to look around. It was too dark to see much, but he could tell they stood on a hill. Down below, firelight flickered from numerous spots—like the torches and cooking fires of a village, though larger than any village he'd ever seen. The noise of some animal he didn't quite recognize broke the stillness now and then. He had the sense that wherever he was, it was a long way from home.

"Sheep," Joseph said.

"What?"

"I can hear sheep. And it looks like a town or something down there, don't you think?"

Zeff shifted his feet. "I don't know what *sheep* is. Or *town*."

"Oh." Joseph wrinkled up his forehead. Where did Zeff come from, anyway? "A sheep is an animal. We raise them for food and their hair—wool—is good for clothes and things. And a town—well, it's a place where many people live together. I've never actually lived in a town myself, unless you count the fortress."

"You know this place then?" Zeff asked.

"I don't think so." Joseph wrapped his arms around himself. "It feels like—a very long time ago."

"A long time ago?" Zeff tried to take that in. Something like the song about the beginning maybe? The creation of all things. But this did not strike him as the beginning. Not with strange animals and a village as big as the town below them. "If we are dead, this is a very strange afterlife."

Joseph laughed for the first time in a long time.

It lightened the awful heaviness in his chest. "Not what I was expecting for sure." He fell silent, and the heaviness returned.

"I don't believe we are dead." Zeff looked back up at the stars. Unfamiliar, yes, but now that he looked, he could pick out the figures he knew. They just weren't in their expected places. The realization comforted his unease.

"What is happening to us?" Joseph asked. Zeff had his head thrown back, gazing at the stars. "Why are we here? How? I kept...I kept seeing you, almost like I was you."

"Yes, it was the same for me." Zeff lowered his eyes from the heavens and the two young men regarded each other by the light of the stars and the crescent moon. Joseph squinted. Despite Zeff's darker skin and hair, they looked remarkably alike.

"It's like we could be brothers," Joseph said.

"What do you mean?" Zeff's heart pinched tight at the thought of his brother.

"We look alike, don't you think? Except for our complexion."

"Do we?" Zeff blinked. He'd never given any thought to what he looked like before. It wasn't as if he could see his own face, after all. "Am I really so pale?" He examined his hand.

"No, no. You're much darker than me. But our faces aren't so different. You don't see it?"

"I have never seen my face, of course."

"You've never looked in a mirror?"

"I don't know what *mirror* is."

"Oh." Joseph had never thought of that. When were mirrors invented anyway? He gasped. "Maybe you're my ancestor."

"Ancestor? How could that be. We are the same age aren't we?" Zeff leaned in closer. "Where do you come from? It is very strange to me."

"I...I think...I think I live a long time from now. In the future. And maybe..." He shrugged. "Maybe you're one my ancestors from long ago."

"But I have no children." He lowered his head. "I couldn't be—"

"Something's happening." Joseph motioned to the sky above them. A spot of light, bigger and brighter than the other stars appeared, growing larger, brighter until Zeff could see the grassy hill on which they stood, and the unfamiliar animals—what had Joseph called them? Sheep?—and the men who appeared to be caring for them. Then the light resolved itself into the form of a man. A man made of light, standing in the sky!

Zeff fell to his knees, covering his head with his hands. What could such a being do to them? He wasn't sure he wanted to find out.

"Wait." Joseph put his hand on Zeff's shoulder. His heart pounded in anticipation. "I know what's happening. It's Christmas. That's the angel. Don't be afraid."

At the same moment the angel's voice echoed over the hillside. "Fear not: for, behold, I bring you good tidings of great joy, which shall be to all people. For unto you is born this day in the city of David a Savior, which is Christ the Lord."

Tears pricked in Joseph's eyes. "It's real," he whispered in awe. He wanted to laugh and dance with delight. "Just like in the Bible."

"Christ the Lord?" Zeff puzzled. "Does that mean the Son of God?"

"Yes, yes. Just watch." Joseph pointed at the sky where one man of light had been now there were many—more people than Zeff had ever seen in his whole life—all of them shining and glorious. They began to sing, the heavenly music filling the quiet night. Zeff gasped. He knew the song. He had heard it on the lips of the singer.

Visions burst upon him as the beings of light sang, more than he could comprehend or contain. When the music stopped, he found he was still on his knees and tears ran freely down his cheeks.

"Let's go see Him," Joseph said.

"See who?"

"The baby Jesus. The Son of God. That's Bethlehem down there."

"We can see Him?" Zeff asked.

"Why not? Look." Joseph pointed to the shepherds moving down the hill in the fading angel light. Nervous excitement pounded in his chest. "We just have to follow them."

Joseph helped Zeff to his feet, and the two of them stumbled down behind the more sure-footed men with their sheep. The air was so different from the forest and seashore of Zeff's home. Cool and dry, dusty enough to cause a tickle in his throat. Joseph gratefully breathed in the night air clean of ash and smoke and despair.

Soon, they came to Bethlehem. Joseph touched the weathered stones of the city walls in awe at their solid reality. He really was here. What a miracle.

Zeff hesitated to pass into a village so big it could hardly be considered a village at all. He shrank from the stone walls and buildings that loomed above him. But Joseph pulled him forward, not wanting to lose sight of the shepherds.

Even at this late hour, the young men had to dodge people and animals wandering the streets. The noise of it rattled against the quiet stillness of the hillside. Zeff grimaced at the smell of so many bodies and animals crowded into the space.

Joseph kept hold of Zeff's arm so they wouldn't get separated. After a few minutes, they came to a section of town less crowded and with fewer lanterns to light the way. The shepherds stopped outside the entrance of a small, stone stable, glowing with the warm light of a lantern within. An aura hung over the place. A feeling of peace, of holiness, that neither Zeff nor Joseph could adequately put into words.

The shepherds moved reverently into the stable, bending at the knee in front of the tiny manger with the baby wrapped in clean, white linens lying inside. The mother and father were there, too. Watching over the newborn child. Joseph stood still in the entrance, his breath caught in his throat. Zeff hovered beside him. "Should we go in?" Joseph whispered.

Zeff didn't answer. He didn't trust his voice to work. Neither of them took a step. Then the mother, Mary, who could not have been any older than Peggy, beckoned them forward.

Zeff stepped in first, with Joseph only a heartbeat behind. They wove through the kneeling shepherds until they stood beside the manger. The baby looked like any ordinary baby to Zeff, warm and wrinkled as an old man with a fuzzy shock of dark hair. But the feeling of holiness that hung around this child marked him as anything but ordinary.

"Would you like to hold him?" Mary asked.

"You don't mind?" Joseph said.

"That's why you came, isn't it?" She picked up the baby Jesus and handed him to Joseph.

He let out his breath, cradling the tiny child in his arms, warm and soft and real. The Christ child, just like he'd read about his whole life. Tears crowded into his eyes. He thought about his own child, who must have come by now. An unexpected peace welled up inside him.

Zeff cupped his hand around the baby's head, feeling the silky softness of his baby hair. Joseph understood all this much better than he did. Question upon question crashed through his mind like waves breaking on the shore, but this was not the right time or place to ask them. Maybe he would not get the chance to ask them before he died. For surely he and Joseph could not stay in this time and place forever. A calm assurance . settled over him. Maybe he did not need to know all the answers. Maybe being here, now, was enough. Zeff touched the tiny hand, and let the baby's fingers wrap tightly around his own. He looked up at Joseph. "The Son of God."

"He really came," Joseph said. A smile spread across his face.

"You mean He will come," Zeff said, focusing on the baby again.

"Yes." The truth of it burst upon Joseph like the sun coming out from behind a dark cloud. "Yes. He will come."

# XIV.

Zeff jerked forward, startled to find his hands still bound around the tree and not cradling the infant Son of God. He groaned. Something rustled behind him, and he tensed. Would his guard even bother saving him from a wild animal?

But it was no animal. He felt a hand on his arm, and someone whispered, "Hold still." A few knife strokes later, the rope dropped from his wrists. He slumped forward, catching himself on numb arms just before he smashed into the forest floor. He waited on his hands and knees for his trembling muscles to regain their strength.

"Can you walk?" His rescuer crouched in front of him.

"Dahlia?"

"Yes, it's me. Can you walk?"

"I think so." He came shakily to his feet. "The guard—"

"Shh. He's asleep."

"How do you know?"

"I've been watching. Shh. Let's go." She pulled him forward into the darkened forest. He stumbled at first, but soon found his footing as the forest began to speak to him again.

They moved swiftly and silently through the trees. Dahlia kept a tight hold on Zeff's hand. He had so much he wanted to ask her, so much he wanted to say, but instead he kept his ears pricked for sounds of pursuit. Though if it were any of Plik's hunting party pursuing them, they likely wouldn't hear it anyway.

After what felt like hours to Zeff's aching legs, Dahlia finally came to a stop. Zeff sank to the ground and rested his head in his hands. The night was fading into dawn. If Plik didn't know Zeff had escaped already, he soon would.

"Do you think they're coming after us?" Dahlia asked.

"Maybe. Hopefully we got a good head start. But Plik's hunters are skilled trackers."

Dahlia bit her lip. "Our trail would be easy for anyone to find."

"Don't worry." Zeff sighed. "I think...I hope...that my being gone will be enough." He traced a pattern in the loam beneath him. "I like to think my father doesn't actually want to see me dead. Besides—" He brushed his hand off on his dirty tunic—"I'm not afraid to die anymore."

"You're not going to die," Dahlia said. "At least, I don't want you to die." She looked at the ground.

"Why did you rescue me?"

"Because I know you didn't kill my father." She drew her knees up to her chest. "You told me you believe what he taught."

"I do." He smiled. "Dahlia, I've seen Him. The Son of God."

"What? When?"

"Last night. Or a long time from now. I don't know. I was there, but not really there." He shook his head, trying to find the words to explain. "I saw Him on the day He was born. Or will be born. I saw Him and touched Him. And I saw his mother, and angels. Oh, the angels." He closed his eyes, remembering the heavenly music and light. "It's kind of a long story."

"You truly saw Him?" Dahlia's face lit up.

Zeff nodded. "I did. I can tell you the whole story, if you like."

"I would." She scooted over closer to him. "Zeff, you should know…my father, the last time he left, he told me he would find a…a husband for me."

"A husband?"

"Yes." She picked a wildflower and rolled it in between her thumb and forefinger. "I know we don't really know each other, but I trust my father's judgment."

"You think he chose me to be your husband?" Something warm and dizzying broke over him at the thought.

"Yes. I mean, only if you want to." She bit her lip and focused intently on the little blossom in her fingers.

Zeff thought of Joseph insisting they were

connected—family. Maybe he was right. Maybe it would start here and stretch onward to the furthest generations. He took her hand. "I would be honored to be your husband."

She smiled, leaned over and kissed him boldly on the mouth. He wrapped his arms around her and pulled her closer. This was certainly better than being executed with the dawn.

Dahlia pulled away from him. "We'd better go. Someone could be coming after us."

"Yes," Zeff said with a pang of regret. He helped Dahlia up, and took her bag full of food and supplies to carry himself for a while. "Where are you taking us?"

"To the mountaintop. You'll see." She grinned, but offered no further explanation.

\* \* \*

Two days later, on the far side of the island from Zeff's village, they came to the top of the highest mountain on the island. From here, Zeff could look down on the forest canopy stretching away in all directions, and beyond that the sea surrounding and encompassing the world. There were other places out there, beyond the sea. He'd seen them and touched them. And there was more to the world than what could be seen and touched. He'd experienced that too.

"Are you ready?" Dahlia asked. She took his

hand and led him over to a rough stone altar. Together they knelt, hands clasped and heads bowed.

Zeff began to pray as Dahlia had taught him, awkwardly at first, not really sure of the words to use, but growing more confident as he continued.

When his prayer ended, he clutched Dahlia's hand tighter. The light brightened around them, far brighter than the sunshine, and in the light stood a figure unknown to Zeff, but achingly familiar at the same time.

"My Lord," Zeff whispered in awe.

# XV.

"Joe? Joe! Wake up."

Joseph opened his eyes, surprised to find Peggy bent over him, tears streaking her face. He tried to lift his hand to touch her, but moving proved impossible. Breathing irritated his seared lungs. A sullen rainfall drizzled over them. "I'm hurt," he rasped.

"I know." Peggy sniffled. She ran her hand over his hair. That's when Joseph noticed the baby strapped to her chest, wrapped in a fabric sling that made Joseph think of the Christ Child laying swaddled in the manger.

"The baby." He tried to move his arm again to touch his child. He almost reached the tiny bald head before his hand dropped.

"Our son." Peggy laughed through her tears. "He's perfect. I named him Michael Tanner after our fathers."

Joseph attempted a smile. Michael Tanner Warren. His son. Perfect.

"He looks like you," Peggy said. "He has your eyes." Her voice broke. Joseph reached for her hand, and she took it gently in hers. "I've been searching for you," she said. "But I had to stop when the baby came."

Joseph squeezed her hand, which sent needles of pain up his arm.

"It was scary giving birth, but I wasn't alone. I mean, I couldn't see anyone else, but I know I wasn't alone. It all turned out fine, but I couldn't look for you anymore. That was two weeks ago."

"I'm sorry," Joseph whispered. "I couldn't...I thought..."

"Shh. You don't have to say anything."

But he did. He had so much to tell her.

"Then I heard the planes and explosions so nearby," Peggy went on. "I had to find out what was happening." She drew in a shuddering breath. "Oh, Joe, thank heavens I found you before..." She trailed off.

"Before I died," Joseph finished for her.

"I don't know what to do for you," Peggy sobbed. "You're hurt bad."

He could tell that, but imminent death didn't seen quite as terrifying anymore. "It'll be okay, Pegs. Help me up. I want to see the baby."

Peggy got her arm under his shoulders and helped him sit up with his back against a boulder. The effort left him gasping for breath. The world had burned. The land was blasted and dead, the air darkened with ash and soot, with the cold rain turning it all into mush.

Peggy sat beside him and unwrapped the baby from her chest. She held him out for Joseph to see. The child lay asleep in his mother's arms. "Michael,"

Peggy whispered, "here's your daddy."

Joseph ignored the pain to reach up and stroke the baby's head. His hand was nearly as burned as the trees. He winced. It must be a miracle that he wasn't dead already. "Hello, baby boy."

The baby's face scrunched up, and then his eyes opened, clear and blue as the sky should have been, and love swallowed Joseph whole.

"You're right. He's perfect."

Peggy laid her head down on Joseph's shoulder. Gingerly, he slid his arm around her. Everything dimmed. He didn't know if his sight was fading or the darkness was increasing. Either way, he knew it wouldn't be long. He felt no fear, only peace and reassurance.

"Oh, Joe, please don't die," Peggy said.

"It will be all right." If only he had the breath and strength to tell her everything he'd seen. "I saw Him, Pegs. He really came, and He's coming again."

"Who?"

"The Lord Jesus."

Peggy gasped. "What do you mean? When did you see Him? When is He coming?"

Joseph wanted to answer, but the darkness had grown complete. He felt each ragged breath in his lungs. Each thump of his heart. He felt Peggy's head still on his shoulder his arm around her. He could hear the baby's soft breathing—all with great clarity.

Was this what death felt like then? To suddenly feel every detail of life so keenly?

A pinprick of light pierced the dark. Joseph wasn't sure if his eyes were open or closed. His heart sped up, joyful anticipation washing over him. The light spread, driving the darkness before it. Peggy's head lifted off his shoulder. He wanted to say goodbye to her, but before he could, the light consumed him.

His pain vanished in an instant. Each breath, each heartbeat, full of life and vitality. He cried out for joy, and to his surprise heard Peggy's delighted laugh beside him. He blinked, and the beautiful brightness dimmed enough for him to see that he and Peggy, with the baby in her arms, stood in a forest glade renewed to its former splendor.

"You were right," Peggy said. "Look."

She pointed to the clouds. Joseph raised his head, and saw Him, descending in glory with a host of angels far greater than those at his birth, singing as they had then, filling the air with their praises.

There were people on the ground rushing toward him too. His parents and Peggy's and a crowd of others he didn't know, and...was that Zeff? Joseph blinked. It was. Zeff grinned and lifted his hand in greeting.

Joseph dropped to his knees, with Peggy beside him. He lifted his arms to the heavens, and shouted hosannas to his Lord and King.